Introduction

This is a unique story about a cuckoo who realises family matters.

The copy rights of this book and story are owned by Dennis John Machin as of 7th March 2021

Written In dedication to

my big sister Sheila Ann Isitt

31st May 1941

-

9th January 2021
Covid victim

Tick-Tock

Written by

Dennis Machin

Chapter one

One spring morning in a wood near a farm and fields, the air was still and the sunlight beamed through the fresh green canopy of the tree tops. In the tree tops were two Robins, Henry and Ruby. They were flying around looking for the perfect spot to make a family home.

As they flew from tree to tree Henry's eye caught a glistening light below them.

"Look at that stream and those fallen tree trunks, that means fresh water and woodlice and bugs for food." As they flew on, they saw the farmer's field. "When the farmer ploughs his field, think of all the juicy worms we could find" Ruby said excitedly.

They both turned to one another and agreed this would be the perfect spot to build their nest.

Ruby flew about the forest searching for little twigs, small but strong, then she clasped mud in her claws which would hold the sticks together. Now nests don't happen overnight so Ruby worked hard for 2 days placing every twig in the perfect position. On the third day she collected moss from tree barks, feathers from the farm and soft fallen leaves to give the nest warmth and comfort. Whilst Ruby was busy building their perfect home Henry flew around the forest finding the best grubs he could, bringing food to Ruby and taking note of the fruit shrubs that would soon be full. On the 3rd night they both snuggled together in their new home and the two tired little robins fell straight to sleep.

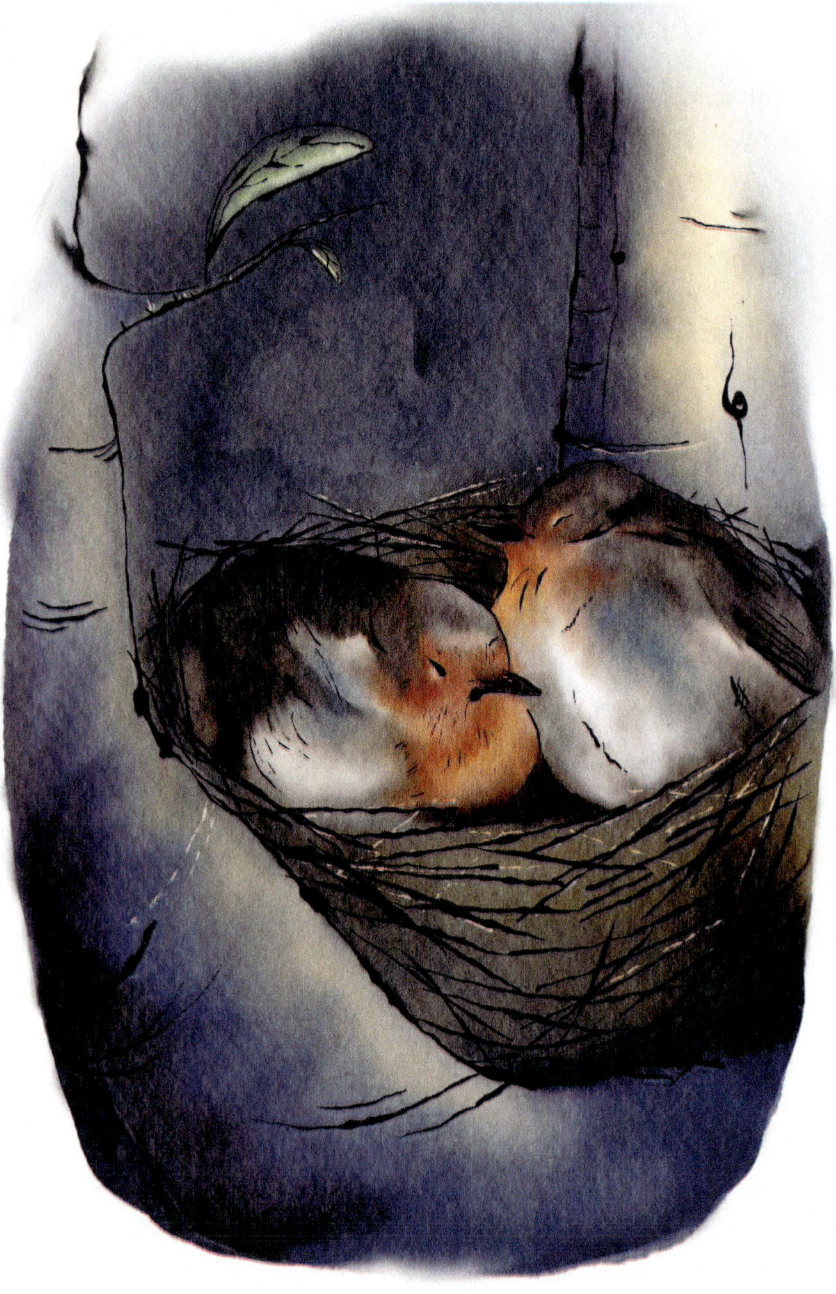

The next few days passed and they settled into their new home. Henry continued to explore the forest and by the end of the week Ruby had a glow about her, she was ready to lay her eggs. Five eggs were laid and a lot of care, love and attention was given to them.

A few trees away Mr and Mrs Cuckoo were watching Henry and Ruby, as they had been for a number of days. Mrs cuckoo was studying their eggs from afar and had finally decided that they were close enough to her own.

"Right, are you ready?" asked Mrs Cuckoo. "Well darling I am still not sure about this" replied Mr Cuckoo.

"What's the matter with you? Can't you see I'm tired after our long journey? Since we flew from Africa, I've been hunting different nests down and I've spent the last few days watching these stupid robins and now I just want to lay my egg "snapped Mrs Cuckoo.

"This must be done, I don't want to be sitting on eggs for weeks! Just think about when they are born. Think how dirty my nails would get digging around for worms and there would be no time to prune my feathers," Mrs cuckoo said, exasperated.

"Please let's get this over and done with right now!".

"Sorry my love" Mr cuckoo stuttered. " You need to scare them off for a while to give me enough time to lay my egg" explained Mrs cuckoo.

Mr cuckoo thought about the plan, it didn't seem right but he didn't want to have to build a nest or go hungry because little ones needed feeding. With this in mind he spread his wings and flew towards the robin's nest with speed and aggression.

"Away with you! Get lost you nasty little creatures!" he growled at the poor robins as he invaded their home.

Henry and Ruby began to attack the nasty Cuckoo, their only thought was to protect their precious eggs at all cost. Mr cuckoo was a lot bigger than the robins and he used this to his advantage charging his beak into their heads and chests. The little robins didn't stand a chance and they knew it. Still, they gave it their all pecking at the cuckoo's chest, tearing out his feathers. They did this until Henry got struck by the cuckoo's powerful wings and went hurling to the ground, Ruby, fearing the worst flew straight down to Henry to see if he was all right. Henry lay there motionless with Ruby's wings wrapped around him in desperation.

Mrs cuckoo who had been watching the nest, flew across to lay her egg. As she landed, she noticed the five eggs. Shaking her head, she knew there was not enough room to lay her egg here. She began kicking them out, sending them crashing to the ground. As she came to the last egg she paused, she thought she had better not get rid of all the eggs, she had to give the robins a reason to stay. Mrs cuckoo nudges the last egg to the side and feeling content that there was enough room for her to comfortably lay her egg she began to do so. Then she flew back to the branch where Mr Cuckoo was waiting.

"My dear, I am worried I may have been too vicious with the robins, what if he does not wake?" Mr cuckoo turned to ask his mate. "The deed is done, if he does not wake then she will raise the eggs alone." Cold hearted Mrs Cuckoo turned away from her husband.

"I've still got 5 more eggs to lay, are you going to help me find another nest or stay here pitying the weak?" she said as she flew away from him. Mr cuckoo followed his mate, thankful that his chicks would at least grow in a loving environment.

Meanwhile back on the ground Henry was still motionless but now soaked in Ruby's tears. Then as if her prayers had been answered Ruby felt a faint tap of Henrys wing.

"Henry, Henry please wake up" she begged, Henry then opened his eyes.

He layed still for a second and then rose to hug his mate. Though he could feel pain he knew nothing was broken and that after a good night's sleep he would feel better.

Ruby and Henry, not caring if it was safe, flew back to the nest and Ruby immediately checked the eggs.

"Oh no" she cried as she saw 3 of her eggs had gone. Henry looked into the nest at the two eggs, "Darling, was this egg always this big? Did it always have those specks?" Henry continued to stare at it, something didn't quite feel right, "Oh, I know what that nasty pair have done, they've given us their egg to raise and feed. Our poor babies lost because of this! Well, no I won't have it I'm not raising this thing,"

Even though Ruby was still in shock, she quickly responded "Wait, no darling, four little ones have been lost already it's not this one fault that it's parents abandoned it." Henry replied "Ruby please, we cannot possibly keep it."

Then Henry stopped to look at her, he could see in her eyes she was heartbroken and yet so determined.

"Yes, we can! We will give it a loving home, this little cuckoo will belong to a kind family, a good family." The certainty in Ruby's voice could not be ignored or compromised with, so Henry said no more on the subject.

Chapter two

Ruby stuck to her intentions. She kept all the eggs that remained in the nest warm and guarded, not letting the precious eggs out of her sight for one second. Two weeks later a Robin appeared and no more than three days after so did the Cuckoo.

By this time, Mr and Mrs cuckoo had laid all their eggs and departed, they had not stuck around to see the birth of any of their chick's. They do not care for their children, not this one or the others that they were abandoning in nests all across the country. This is the being of a cuckoo you see, deserted by their own parents they knew no other way of life.

At the time of the cuckoo's birth Henry was out collecting food for his new born. When He returned he landed on the edge of the nest, looked inside and was shocked to see the size of the chick.

"Ruby, look at the size of the bird compared to ours, it's going to take a whole lot of feeding, are you sure you want to do this? After all it's not our responsibility" Henry said. "Yes of course, we will rise to this challenge with ease, there are two of us and two of them, it will be fine" Ruby replied with a firm tone looking at her two cherubs. "Yes, we will" Henry said clearly not as confident. "Looking at this creature I have no idea what its name could be, well at least not a nice name for it" Henry told Ruby "Now now Henry, do not be so cruel we will not have a favourite they are both our children now, as for his name we will send them both to the owl. The owl is wise and will give our children good, strong names, until then they will be, hmm, Robin and Cuckoo." Ruby responded, with certainty in her voice. Though Henry was right, she still felt such love towards the poor abandoned cuckoo.

As the weeks went by the two brothers grew closer, not just as brothers but in the literal sense and Cuckoo amused by the tininess of his big brother bestowed upon him the nick name Titch. See his mother had treated him with such love, ignoring the fact he was probably almost five times the size of all of them all. So, though Cuckoo knew he was different he also knew he had a family that loved him dearly and that he loved too. That being said, brothers will be brothers and brothers often fight.

"Honestly bro, can't you move over a bit I am about to fall out here" said the little robin. "I'm sorry Titch, let me try and move to the left a bit" Cuckoo replied feeling bad for squashing his brother.

Cuckoo shuffled to the left as much as he could, until his wings were pushed right up against the side of the nest.

"Is that better Titch?" he asked. "Thank you, that is a bit better, now I actually have space to breathe." "You know I can't help it Titch" sighed Cuckoo." "Yes, but you can help eating all the worms that Mum and Dad bring back!" "That's true, I will let you have first pick next time, I promise, I was just so hungry last night" Cuckoo said, trying to justify his greediness.

Cuckoo took a look at his brother and began to think about how unalike they were, not just in size but also in personality.

"Compared to you I am so big, have you ever wondered why we are so different?" asked Cuckoo. "I told Mum and Dad not to get those worms by the nuclear power station, they must have given you a radioactive worm and It has affected your growth, you're what they call a mutant" Titch spattered between laughs. "Shut up Titch, you're worrying me now" huffed Cuckoo. "You know what else I've noticed, I have this feeling in my bones, like I'm not going to be here forever, like I'm meant to see the world." Cuckoo said dreamily. "Bro look around, there are plenty of trees, water and good food, why leave? I doubt you will find somewhere as good as this" Titch replied, quite content with his lifestyle and surroundings. "I guess I just got itchy feet then" Cuckoo said with a smile. "Well wouldn't it just be easier to scratch them?" Titch responded in a rather smug manner.

Cuckoo suddenly jolted "Ow! Ow my leg! It is all cramped up!" he cried. "Well stretch it out a bit then, that will help" advised Titch, who hopped onto the nest edge to give his brother more room.

The cuckoo did as his brother suggested and it had a devastating consequence. He stretched his leg as far as he could until he hit the sides of the nest, then he heard a scream.

"Oh no" he cried stretching his neck up looking for Titch. "Titch, Titch" he called, "Where are you Titch?" He looked over the edge of the nest and felt sick as tears began to soak his feathers. "Bro I'm here at the bottom of this fern. I think something's broken, I'm in such unbelievable

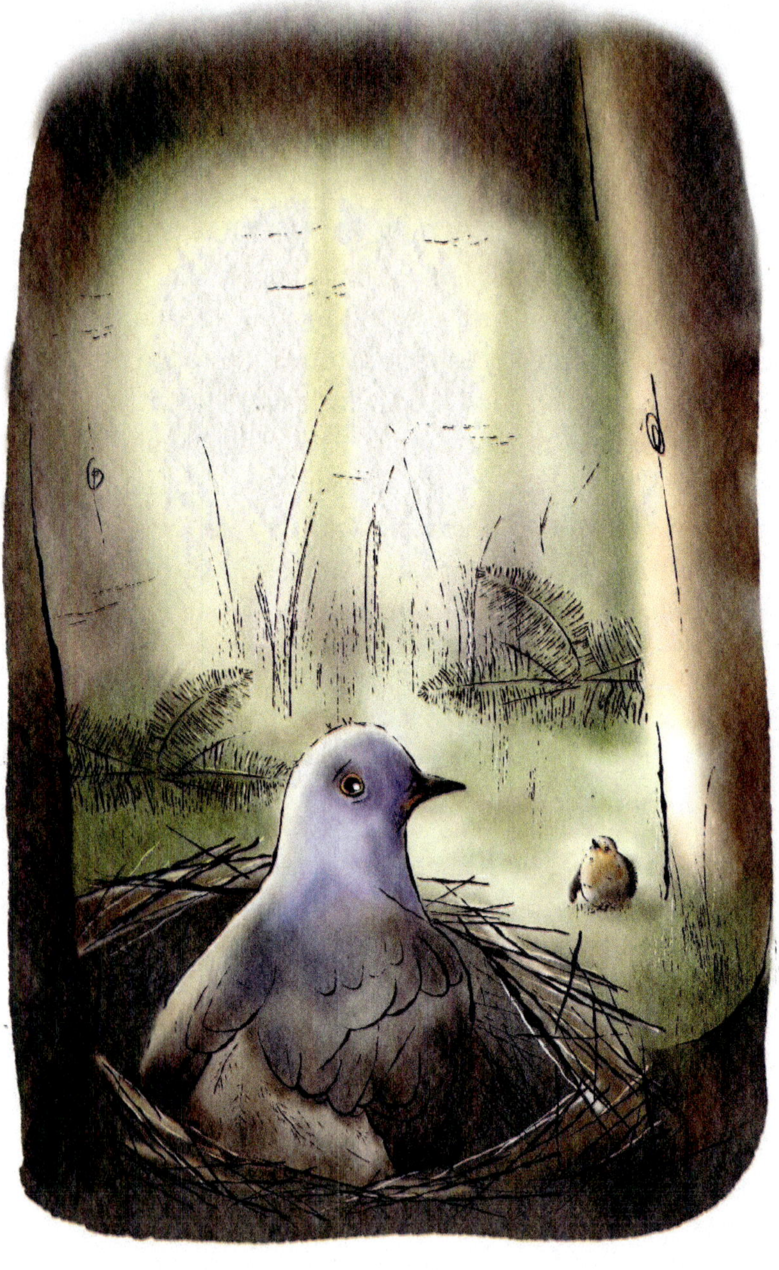

pain" Titch sobbed looking up at his home, which now seemed so very far way. "Okay, it's going to be okay. Mum and Dad will be back soon, just don't move". Cuckoo said as reassuringly as he could. Titch lay on the ground in agony, making sure he didn't move a muscle as he waited for his parents.

Chapter three

"Fritz. Why have you stopped" Sky said looking at the dog, he had set his body in a rather odd position. It's tail, back, neck and head all in a straight line pointing towards a bush. Sky had noticed this stance before when she was out with her father to shoot pigeons. Her father had told her that's why they were called German pointers, because they point to where the birds are. Sky went over to the bush curious at what the dog had spotted, she started rummaging through the leaves and then she saw the frightened little robin.

"Oh, you poor thing" she cried as she scooped the little robin up in her hands as gently as possible. Fritz who was watching her intently stepped forward sniffing Sky's arms, "good boy Fritz, well spotted" she praised.

As she examined the bird, she thought she could see a break in the wing, whilst thinking to herself about what to do she looked up, searching for a nest or perhaps the robin's parents. Sky did see a nest but from this she heard a cuckoo's call, not a robin. So Sky decided, as the bird was injured, she would take it back to the farm where she lived with her Mother and Father. Her dad was a farmer, if anyone knew how to take care of animals it was him. She began to rush home calling for Fritz to follow.

When Sky reached the farmhouse, she rushed through the back door frantically.

"Mummy, mummy, look what I have found!" she cried with her hands held out "Oh Sky, what have I told you about charging in here, you gave me such a fright!" Sky's mother replied rather crossly. She walked towards her daughter to look at what had agitated her so much. "Poor little love, what have you done to yourself" she turned to Sky and said "It is definitely a broken wing, you were right to bring it home with you." Sky's mother began to think of what she would need as she looked down at the fragile, clearly petrified, robin. "Okay Sky, go find me a shoe box, some cotton wool, scissors and some tape. Oh and get an ice lolly from the freezer and eat it."

Sky did as she was told rushing about the house trying to remember if she had left the scissors in her craft box. As Sky hurried about the house, her mother nursed the little robin, trying to calm it down and reassure it as best she could. Ten minutes later Sky appeared in the kitchen, out of breath buth with her arms full.

"Everything you asked for Mum" Sky said as she placed everything on the table.

She took the robin from her mum and watched her create a little home. As instructed, Sky put the bird in the box carefully. She stood there with her lolly watching as the little robin hobbled about curiously.

"Mum, why did I need to eat a lolly?" Sky asked, now holding a wooden stick in her hand. "I'm going to take the stick, clean it and then use it to make a splint for the wing love. Just leave it on the table" her mother replied. "Oh okay, that's clever. Mum I'm going to run up to the field and tell dad about the bird, I won't be long" Sky explained as she walked out the door. "Bring him back with you, our dinner will be done soon" Her mother shouted after her.

Sky ran to the fields where she found her father herding in the cows. She watched patiently, waiting for the last one to head into the barn, then she called him over. As they walked back to the farm she began to describe her exciting day, telling him all about the poor little bird she had saved.

"That smells good, I'm so hungry!" Sky and her dad both muttered as they walked through the back door with a rumbling tummies. "Sheila, what you got cooking that smells so good?" Bernie asked, "Classic beef wellington with some veggies, it ought to put some strength back into you after your days work Bernie" she replied, "It won't be done for another five minutes though, could you take look at the little bird? I'm pretty sure it's got a broken wing" Shelia said as she filled up the kettle.

Bernie sat down at the table sliding the box towards him so he could take a better look.

"Sky, pick him up carefully for me so I can get a better look at the wing, poor thing won't move out the corner it's so scared" Bernie whispered, not wanting to frighten the bird even more. Sky did as she was told, picking up the bird as carefully as she could. "Hmm little one, what did you do to yourself? Took a jump out of nest too soon and fell I'm guessing" Bernie muttered to the robin. "I have a lollipop stick, mum said you could use it to make a splint for his broken wing" Sky said as she handed her dad the stick.

Sheila with two cups in her hand sat down at the table, placing one of the cups by Bernie. After taking a sip he looked to his mate and said "this tea is a bit strong Sheila." "Well my lover, pick the mug up with two hands" she replied. Bernie smiled at Sheila. "ha ha, just a bit more milk please" to which Sheila obliged.

"Break the lollipop stick in half cos were going to place it on both sides of the wing. Sheila, you hold the wing out, Sky, you're going to put the sticks in place and I will tape it up" Bernie said after taking a gulp of his now not so strong tea.

The robin, which was a lot calmer now as Sky had been softly stroking it, was given to Sheila while Sky very quickly put the wooden sticks where her father instructed and held them tight in place. Bernie then tried to tape it up.

"This is not working, the tape is not working. I think it's the feathers, it just won't stick to them." Bernie said frustrated.

He was trying to think of what to do, looking around the kitchen for an idea when he noticed the draw Sheila kept her sewing things in. Bernie went to the draw, grabbed a needle and thread and as he sat down at the table again, he tried to thread the needle, this required all his concentration.

"Dad, your tongue is sticking out, what are you doing?" Sky said trying not to giggle as she was still holding the splints.

After the hundredth attempt, he got the thread through the needle, still concentrating, he poked the needle into the robin's feathers and then around the stick. He kept going through the feathers and all around the two sticks until they were tight and secure against the robin's wings.

"That ought to do it, you can put the bird back in the box now Sheila" Bernie said as he tied a knot in the thread and put the needle down. "He was a right little fidget, had to keep hold of him tight I did, I'm surprised he didn't do himself more harm," Sheila said as she gently folded the wing into the robin's body.

She gave the robin back to Sky who began to stroke him again hoping to keep him calm.

"How long will he need the splints on?" Sky asked. "I'd say at least four weeks" Sheila answered as she cleared up the cups and got some plates out. "Sky, you had best put him in the box and come and wash your hands" Bernie instructed, walking towards the sink. "You're going to have to wake up early to get him lots of worms and you must always keep fresh water in the box for him. As you brought him home, he will be your responsibility darling" Bernie explained to his daughter. "Has it got to be early? I'm sure there will be lots of worms about all day long" Sky answered. "Have you never heard about the early bird catching the worms? Best worms are up at sunrise and this little one will need the biggest worms out there to get strong and healthy again" Bernie told his daughter. "Okay dad" Sky sighed, she was happy she helped the poor bird but was also a big fan of her bed, being up before sunrise didn't sound much fun.

"Bernie, do you reckon it will heal up okay?" Sheila asked her husband as she placed a plate of steaming food in front of him. "Well, I'm not sure, he is a bit small, It's like he was always the last of the litter to eat, but if he was practising flying then that means he was getting ready to leave the nest. I think with a good helping of food and some rest he may heal up nicely" Bernie answered. Sheila sat down at the table and they all tucked into the yummy food.

After dinner, the family went about doing their own thing. Sky had some maths homework due in for school so she went off to her room, Sheila set about cleaning the kitchen and Bernie perched on the sofa with a paper, relaxing after his long day. As the night became darker the family came together and sat around the living room watching some TV until it was eventually bed time. Sky went to observe the little robin, curious of whether the creature had settled and calmed after the earlier commotion.

She approached the box slowly and just watched the robin as it hopped out the box getting water and pecking at the breadcrumbs she had left. "Little robin, I want to name you" she said quietly. She thought to herself that maybe Lucky would be an appropriate name as he was lucky to be found by her and not a nasty animal. However, that seemed very conventional and typical Sky thought for a while, staring at robin, noticing its pruned feathers so clean

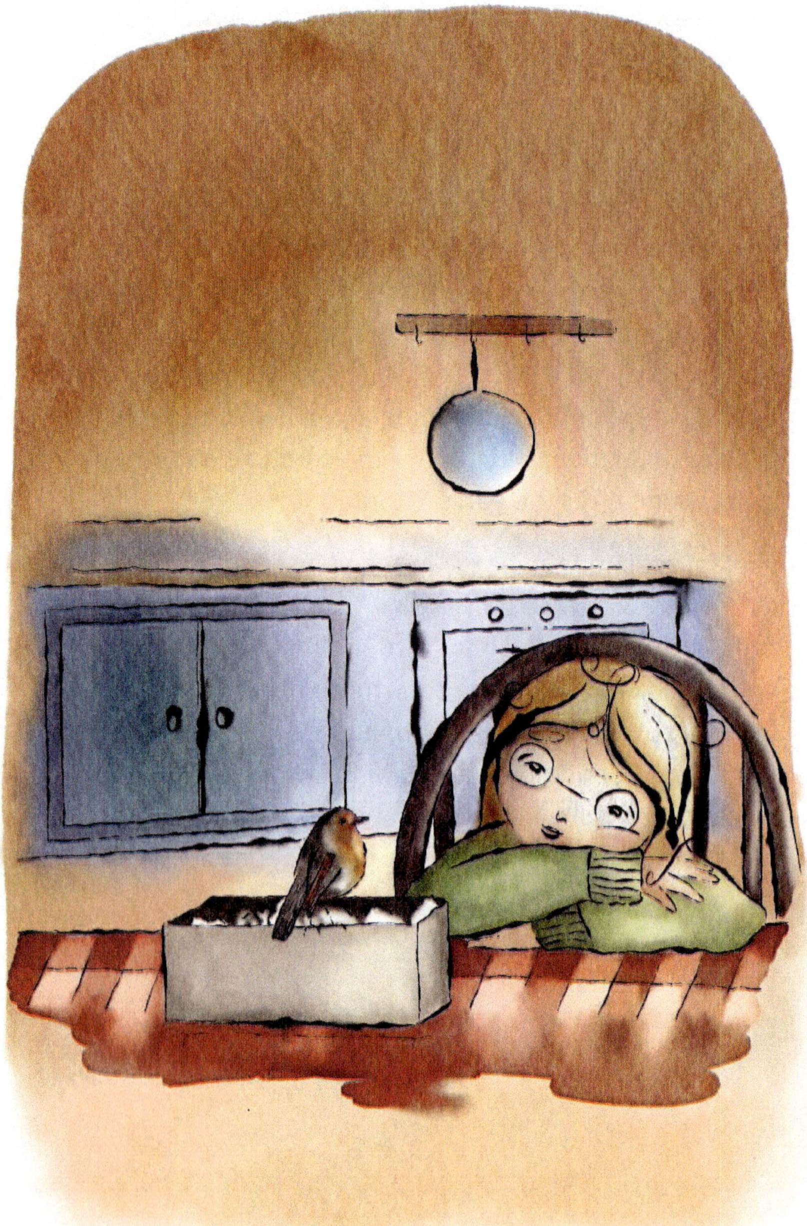

"What will you call it Sky?" Sheila asked. "Robin, my little Robin." Sky stated. "That's a lovely name love, its bed time now so say goodnight and off you pop" Sheila said putting the last of the cups in the cupboard.

The lights went off and footsteps could be heard as the family went upstairs to sleep. Titch looked around the room and began to feel very lonely, missing his family and home. Though the child, a fair girl with blonde hair and eyes so blue they really did represent a morning sky, had brought him to this alien place and her companions had poked and prodded his wing causing immense pain, he did feel as though it was not better but more stable and the pain had somewhat subsided. They had also created a comfy little abode for him to rest and showed him love, caressing him when he felt so frightened.

Titch had looked around the room earlier in the day, when he had first entered, it was nothing like the forest he came from. This room had a yellow sort of hue to it and though there were some trees, they were very odd and not at all what he was used to. In fact they came in a completely different shape and he had seen they were full of strange items. Titch fell asleep that night very unsure of his surroundings and whether or not he was truly safe, but his last thought was of his family which led to his sleep being a peaceful one.

Chapter 4

Back at the nest Henry and Ruby arrived with their beaks full of food. "Where is your brother?" Henry asked with a worried tone. "It was an accident, I had cramp and Titch fell, there was a girl and a dog and I tried to tell her I did, I screamed and shouted at her to leave Titch alone" Cuckoo stammered choking on his tears. "Hun, calm down, breathe and explain what happened" Ruby said trying to mask the fear in her voice.

Cuckoo took a deep breath and tried to stop his tears, for the past few hours he had barely stopped crying and felt sick every time he thought of Titch.

"Mum and Dad, I'm so sorry, it was just a huge accident! I had cramp in my leg so Titch hopped up on the edge of the nest to give me some room to stretch it out. Then I heard him scream, I called out for him, I shouted his name, I was so scared, I thought maybe….maybe he might have died" Cuckoo explained barely breathing trying to control his emotions again. "Then Titch called up, he said his wing was really painful and he was so upset, crying his eyes out. I didn't know how to help so I told him to stay as still as he could and that you would be home soon." Cuckoo wiped away his tears.

"There there love, it wasn't your fault" Ruby said embracing the cuckoo in her arms.

"So where is your brother now? Who is this girl you mentioned and a dog, what dog Cuckoo?" Henry demanded his voice angry and fearful.

"There was dog about five minutes after Titch fell and well, it pointed towards Titch with its body. Then a girl came along and rummaged through the ferns that Titch had fallen in and she picked him up. I was watching and when I saw that she had him I screamed at her, I told her to leave him alone and I kept shouting and shouting until my throat was sore. She looked up at me, she saw me but she didn't care, she just stole Titch away!" Cuckoo answered angrily.

"Right, okay Cuckoo, this girl, did you see where she went? Where she took Titch?" Ruby asked.

"Yes, she headed straight down that road, I didn't take my eyes off her. She went all the way down, just kept on going straight" Cuckoo replied with certainty.

"Okay, Henry that's where the farm is isn't it? It's straight down the road. Maybe it's the farm girl, Oh, I don't know! What will we do?" Ruby questioned her husband afraid for her poor little chick.

"Mum, I'm going to get Titch back, I will fly down the road, I will go to farm, I will go anywhere to find Titch and bring him home!" Cuckoo stated.

"You're going to find him? You don't even know how to fly! This whole thing could have been avoided Ruby, right from the start I said to you I would fix it! But no, you wanted to be the samaritan and now look where it has got us!" Henry shouted angrily.

"Henry, shouting and arguing is not going to fix any of this, what you are saying is horrible. This was an accident, nothing more. Chicks have accidents they play and they fall, it was the girl who took our baby away and that is not cuckoos fault" Ruby replied sharply.

"I can fly, I've been practicing for days, every time you go to get food, I've been building up my strength. I bet I can even fly all the way to that tree. I'm going to, I'm going to show you right now what I can do!"

Cuckoo hopped onto the edge of the nest and jumped.

"Cuckoo no! Henry, what have you done!" Ruby exclaimed diving after Cuckoo.

27

He fell before he flew that's for sure, he actually thought he might crash into the ground and started flapping with more strength and speed but he did it. All that was going through his mind was Titch, he couldn't let him down not after what had happened. It was an accident but it was an accident caused by him and now he had to fix it.

"That's it Cuckoo! Keep flapping your wings and remember to breath properly" His mum shouted from underneath him. At least she has faith in him, Cuckoo knew both his parents loved him very much, he also knew his dad would never love him the way he loved Titch, his own son. Finally, after what seemed like hours he reached the oak tree opposite his nest. Cuckoo was out of breath and his chest was beating up and down so fast it was a blur. Ruby, content that her son did in fact have the strength to fly went back to the nest.

"Henry, that poor chick looks to you as his hero, I know he's not our own but we made a commitment to love him and raise him, you must forgive him for this" Ruby told Henry.

"I know you're right, I do love him, I loved watching him grow from the day he hatched but I love our Titch too and now he is who knows where. I know I was harsh on him, I'm just scared, so scared Ruby" Henry replied, his eyes were sad and his head low with the shame of how he had spoken to his son.

"I understand and so will Cuckoo, go over to him and talk" Ruby said.

With that, Henry took off towards to the oak tree. He and Cuckoo had a long chat, Henry assured his son of his love reminding him that it was something he would always have. For Cuckoo it was a talk that meant the world, he assured his dad that he would get stronger and he would find Titch. He would do it not just because of his guilt for the accident but because there was no one he loved more than his little big brother and his brother belonged at home.

"Ruby, I do have faith in Cuckoo but he may take weeks to strengthen his wings, should we not go and find Titch ourselves?" Henry asked concerned.

"I understand what you're saying dear, I'm worried too. Cuckoo mentioned a girl though, if it is the girl from the farm then I feel Titch will be okay. I have heard the animals talking about her before, they say she helps her dad take care of them. They say she is a nice, kind child." Ruby replied with a confident tone.

"Well at least that's something I guess, a girl is definitely a lot better than a fox." Henry responded.

"Yes, it most certainly is. Cuckoo loves his brother and he will track him down, until then I will listen out for any gossip amongst the barn animals. We had best get some sleep now, got worms to dig in the morning" Ruby yawned. Both her and Henry snuggled against each other and fell asleep.

Chapter five

As the days went by Cuckoo practiced flying every spare second that he had. He flew from tree to tree, high into the sky and then all the way back down to the ground. Every night he would go to sleep with aching wings but he didn't mind, it was all for his brother who he missed very much.

About two weeks went by and Cuckoos confidence went through the roof. Yesterday he even dared to do a few tricks in the air. Today however, was a more important day because today he would find his brother. The sun rose, lighting up the forest and waking up Cuckoo, he had thought hard about his plan over the past days and now it was time to put it into action.

Cuckoo stretched his wings out and jumped from the nest, heading down the dirt road towards the farm. It was not a long journey but after an hour or so of flying he came to a stream at the edge of the farm. He flew down and guzzled water down his throat. It was the peak of summer, the days were very hot and his journey had left him very dehydrated. As he composed himself, he started to look around for….. well he didn't know what he was looking for, maybe a clue or anything that would guide him to Titch.

Cuckoo began to hear laughter and out of the shrubs tumbled a family of rabbits. Cuckoo watched the family play, there were three little rabbits and their parents. The larger of the adults watched cautiously over the family whilst the other cuddled and caressed the little ones. After a few minutes of watching the family, Cuckoo felt it was safe enough to talk to them so he made his approach.

"Hello there, I was wondering if maybe I could ask for your help? I'm looking for my brother and thought maybe you had seen him? He goes by the name of Robin, or Titch, that's my nickname for him."

"Daisy, Gus, Bella, behind your father please" said the mother rabbit.

Father rabbit stood tall on his large back legs and spoke in a low strong tone "What is your name cuckoo? What is it you need?" father rabbit asked.

"Urm well, my parents call me Cuckoo but I guess you can call me Bruv if you like. What I need is help please, to find my brother" replied Cuckoo.

"Your brother? You said Robin was his name or Titch?" said mother rabbit.

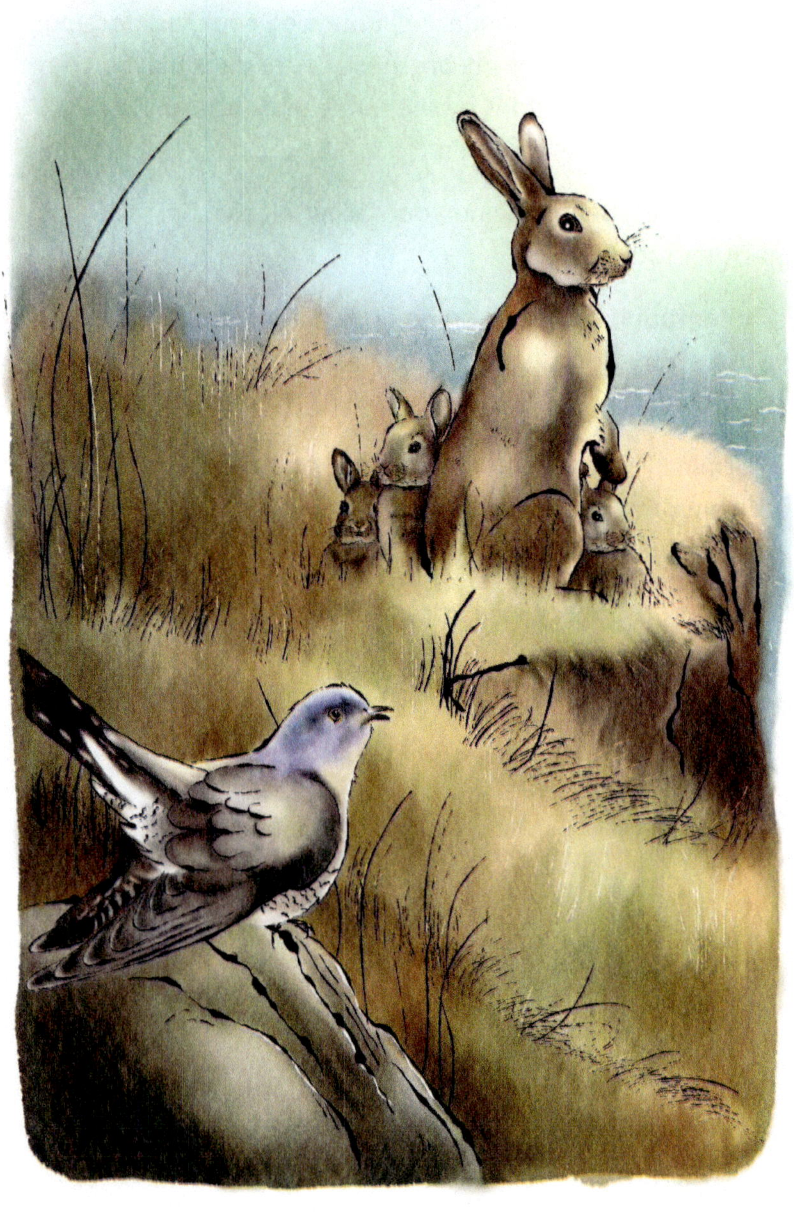

"Yes, that's him, he will answer to both those names. He is small with brown feathers. Apart from his chest that is, those feathers are red" answered Cuckoo.

"Your parents named you as you were then, hmm that's rather odd" mother rabbit thought out loud.

This thought confused Cuckoo but rather than question it he decided to ask again about his brother.

"So, Sir, Miss have you seen my brother or do you know where he could be?" Cuckoo asked.

"My name is Alan and my mates name is Gina and we have not seen your brother I'm afraid"

"I've heard of a robin, I have" Gus called from behind.

"Yes, me too" Daisy shouted.

The three small little rabbits hopped around their father and stood in front of Cuckoo.

"The farm animals spoke of Fritz and a little bird" said Gus.

"Fritz, have you been around the farm where that beast lives?" Gina asked frantically.

"It's okay my love, I was with them, you know I would never let a thing hurt my children, I would defend them with my life and my strong back legs" Alan said as he thumped them on the ground.

"Fritz? What is a Fritz? The last I saw my brother he was taken by a girl and a dog." Cuckoo questioned.

"Fritz is the dog, it's just as well Sky was with him or your brother would have been lunch" Gina explained.

"Lunch? What, oh no, poor Titch" Cuckoo cried

"No Mr Cuckoo, Titch is okay, Sky has him in the house."

"Yes, that's what we heard, the little girl is keeping him safe inside."

"The farm animals said they saw him."

"Very small he was"

"Hence the name Titch I suppose" said the three little rabbits talking quickly over each other.

Cuckoo tried to take in what the rabbits were saying but he felt overwhelmed and confused so he took a deep breath.

"Okay, so my brother is okay? Sky has him? Could just one of you tell me what direction do I go to find him?" He asked whilst looking at Alan.

"Yes, fly up and then left you'll know you're close when you see the pigs" Alan answered.

"See the pigs, you'll smell them first" a little rabbit giggled.

"Thank you for your time and thank you for your help!" Cuckoo replied and then he took to the air.

The cuckoo flew and after a while came to a tree to pause and take a breath. He perched and looked around. All of a sudden he noticed a smell, then he saw it, a pen with a pig and eight little ones running around her. So Cuckoo flew down and landed on a post of her pen.

"Excuse me mother pig, I am looking for my brother. He is a little Robin, goes by the name of Titch, have you seen him?" Cuckoo asked.

The mother pig ignored Cuckoo, he wasn't sure if she had heard him or perhaps she was just busy. One by one she called her young over to bathe them, giving each one as much attention as the other. Cuckoo watched fondly, seeing the love their mother had for them and watching them giggling and play as a family. Eventually the mother pig gave her last young a bath and so Cuckoo tried again

"Mother pig? Excuse me, have you seen a little robin around the farm?" He called out loudly.

"What is your name bird?" The pig asked out of curiosity.

"Urm well, you can call me Cuckoo or you could call me Bruv" Cuckoo replied.

"Cuckoo? That's simplistic, well no Cuckoo, I have not seen your little robin, but I have heard the chicken speak of one at the farm." the mother pig replied and then went back to her young.

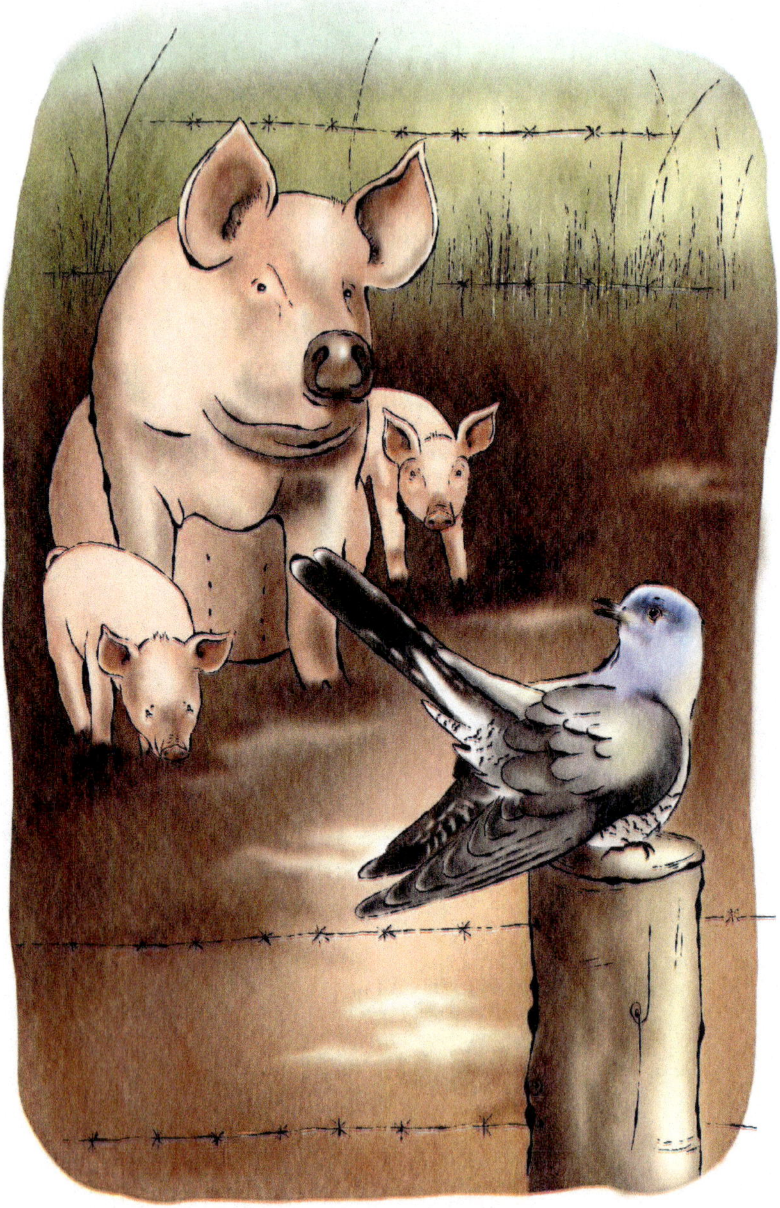

Cuckoo wasn't sure how to respond so flapped his wings and flew over to the barn doors where a chicken and her two chicks were scratching and pecking at the ground.

"Hello mother hen, I am looking for my brother a little robin, have you seen him?" Cuckoo asked.

The chicken sighed but did not stop digging "bird, I am busy, my chicks are hungry, go to the farmhouse for the robin."

"Oh, thank you" replied Cuckoo, he then flew over to the farmhouse and landed on the edge of a window sill. Cuckoo looked into the window to see a kitchen with a little girl sitting at a table with a box.
"A little girl!" He thought to himself, "the little girl?" Cuckoo sat and watched her, she had her hand in the box and it was moving, he was quite confused but sat and waited. After a while the girl got up and collected a box from the cupboard, she then put her hand back in the box and took Titch out and placed him on the table. Cuckoo stared feeling so much joy, his brother was right there! Cuckoo could see that Titch's wing had some kind of bandage on it but he looked happy, the girl was giving him some water and worms from the box. She was stroking his head and watching him lovingly. Cuckoo was so happy to see Titch was okay and being looked after properly. He stayed and watched a while longer then flew back to tell his parents the good news.

Chapter 6

On his arrival, he found Henry and Ruby busy cleaning and tidying the nest.

"Mum, Dad, I found Titch, I found Titch…..he's doing alright!" Cuckoo said excitedly. Ruby looked up at the Cuckoo "Well done son, I am so proud of you! Tell us more, where did you find him?"

"I went to the farm and met lots of different animals, I flew over to the farm house and was lucky to land on the kitchen window sill and there inside was Titch!" Cuckoo explained."

"Well done my boy." Henry exclaimed proudly.

"I saw Titch, a girl was feeding him, he has a broken wing but the humans are taking care of him" Cuckoo continued.

Honestly Cuckoo, you have done so well in finding Titch, you must be hungry, have some worms and relax for the evening" Henry told him.

So Cuckoo perched himself down and began munching on some worms whilst thinking about his day.

"Mum, can I ask you something?" Cuckoo said turning to Ruby. "Of course, what is on your mind dear?" Ruby responded.
"Well when I met the different animals today they asked my name and well, they seemed to think it was simplistic and odd. Why is my name odd?" Cuckoo asked. "Ah well, we wanted you to have good names, strong names" Henry said. "So, we were going to let the owl name you, and until

then thought Cuckoo and Robin would do." Ruby answered. "However, when your brother fell, we were distracted and we forgot about it." Henry continued. "If you don't want to be Cuckoo anymore then fly over the big oak by the wind turbine, that's where the owl lives. Fly there early tomorrow morning just before the sun comes up and ask him to name you." Ruby told Cuckoo.

So the next morning before the sun came up Cuckoo flew over to the edge of the woods by the wind turbine and looked for the large oak where the owl lived. Scanning up and down the different oaks he finally saw a little hole with a little owl perched inside, and flew over.

"Hello, my mum and dad sent me to see you and ask you to give me a name Mr Owl." Cuckoo announced.

"Well, let me see…you are a Cuckoo…hmm." The owl sat there thinking. "You know humans have special clocks, clever things they are, they call them Cuckoo clocks. Your name should be Tick-Tock" the owl said with certainty.

"Tick –Tock? Hmm I like it, Tick-Tock, yes I think it's quite nice" Tick-Tock responded.

"Is there anything else you want to know?" asked the owl. "Well, there is something I want to know, I am a cuckoo but my family are robins, how is this possible Mr Owl?" Tick-Tock asked.

"Ah well Tick-Tock, the first thing to remember is that you are loved by these robins and they will always be your family. The bird that laid your egg was a cuckoo and you won't be the only cuckoo to be left with other birds. You probably have lots of brothers and sisters

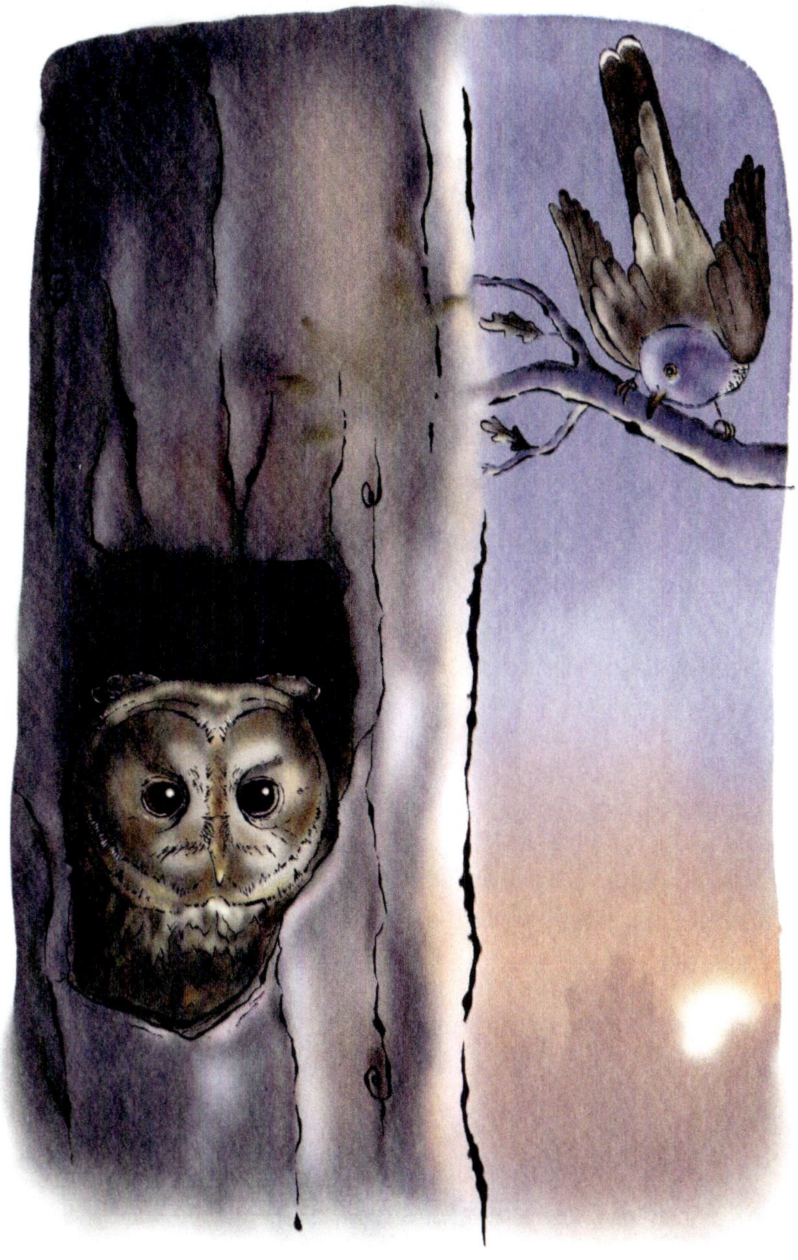

being raised around the country by different birds." the Owl replied.

"But why? At the farm all the animals were with their parents, they were so cute spending family time together. They fed them and bathed them and loved them, just as my parents have done with me and Titch." Tick-Tock said.

"That's just what cuckoos do. They lay their eggs in different nests and then the go to Africa where its warm. They spend time there relaxing and then they find a mate and come back to England from Spring til Winter. When it turns colder they will go again and so repeat the cycle." The owl explained.

Tick-Tock sat there saddened and shocked. Why would a parent just abandon their babies? He sat there and decided right then that wasn't going to be him, he was raised with love and one day he was going to raise his little ones with love too.

"I am a cuckoo, but I will not be that cuckoo. I am going to be different" Tick-Tock told the owl stubbornly.

The owl leaned towards Tick-Tock, closer and closer until his head appeared detached from his body, it made Tick-Tock feel uneasy, then he pulled his head back.

"You are a curious little thing but it is in a cuckoo's nature to abandon their young, it's in your DNA," the owl told him.

"Do you not think someone can change if they really want to? If they really mean it?" Asked Tick-Tock.

"Well, there is the question of If a leopard can change its spots, and I would say the answer is no. But it is in a dogs nature to chase a cat and I have seen the two animals be best of friends. I have heard of lions tamed to see humans as family and not food. The mind is an interesting thing and your upbringing has helped shape who you are, perhaps nurture will overcome nature and perhaps you will choose your own destiny." The owl responded in a calm and all-knowing manner.

"I will choose my destiny and I will choose what type of cuckoo I will be" Tick-Tock said firmly.

"You may choose to be a different bird but you will need to go to Africa to find a mate that thinks like you and that will be hard. You can change who you are but you cannot change others you see. You may explain to them the pros and cons but ultimately it has to be them that make that decision and choose to be different, I think that will be your biggest challenge. The last thing I will say to you is this….a relationship will be hard work, raising your eggs will be even harder, it will be about compromise as well as sacrifice and working as a team. Good luck and goodbye Tick-Tock." The owl said and then turned its head and went to sleep.

Tick-Tock hovered for a second and then flew back home.

Chapter 7

"So, what do we call you, what name has the owl bestowed upon you?" Ruby asked excitedly. "Tick-Tock, I am a cuckoo and the humans have a clever clock named after me" Tick-Tock explained. "You were there for some time Tick-Tock, the owl doesn't normally take so long to name young" Henry said.

"Well, we spoke about other things, we spoke about me being a cuckoo and what that means. I've always had this feeling, to want to fly away and travel, the owl said that in the winter cuckoo's go to Africa for the sun. We spoke about this family, I understand I am different, I know now I was abandoned here, so thank you to both of you for the love you have shown me, the kindness and warmth I have been so fortunate to grow up with, I have decided one day I will do the same. The owl says this is not who I am but I get to choose who I am and I want to be kind, caring and loving, like you, not like my real parents who could just leave me here without a second thought." Tick-Tock explained.

"Oh sweetie, we are so proud of you, of who you have grown up to be. We love you so much and always have and one day you are going to be a great parent." Ruby said warmheartedly with tears in her eyes. "Yes, you will." Henry agreed.

"To be a parent I do need to go though, I need to find a mate and hope they agree with me. The owl said it is our nature as cuckoos to abandon our young, so I need to find a mate and explain to them what a joy it will be to have a family. However, I cannot force them to change, it must be their choice. I will need to be a good partner and show them that I will be a good dad and together we can have a beautiful family." Tick-Tock told them.

"You're leaving soon aren't you? It's slowly starting to get colder, is your instinct to leave getting stronger?" Ruby asked.

"It has been but I could never have left without knowing if Titch was okay. Now I do, I will eat and gather up some strength and then in a few days I'll be going." Tick-Tock answered.

"We understand son, I will help you and show you the best spots to find worms and the best berry shrubs so you can really eat well these next few days" Henry told his Tick-Tock.

So over the next few days Tick-Tock ate and slept. He snuggled up to his parents and enjoyed this time they had together, not knowing if or when he would return or if he would ever get to see them again.

Chapter 8

The day came for him to leave and Tick-Tock knew he had a long and arduous journey ahead of him so he hugged his parents and took off. For days he flew, stopping only for a few hours a day to nap and eat. It seemed like forever but finally he knew he was close, he was almost in Africa.

Tick-Tock stopped and perched on a branch near a watering hole feeling tired and thirsty, he flew down to a log in the water to take a drink. Tick-Tock gulped down some water and took some deep breaths trying to relax. Though the water had quenched his thirst he felt uneasy like something was... SNAP, SNAP, SNAP! The log had suddenly become a crocodile or maybe it had always been a crocodile. Tick-Tock flew high into the air as fast as his wings would take him, his heart beating rapidly as he flew away. Tick-Tock flew as far as his lungs would allow him and then he landed on a tree to try and catch his breath.

"What is this place?" he thought to himself, certainly not England! He knew he was going to need his wits about him if he wanted to make it to Africa, let alone back home. With his heart still pounding Tick-Tock decided to stay for the night. Although he was as comfy as he could be the crocodile had given him quite a scare and Tick-Tock spent most of the night staring at the star suddenly feeling quite home sick.

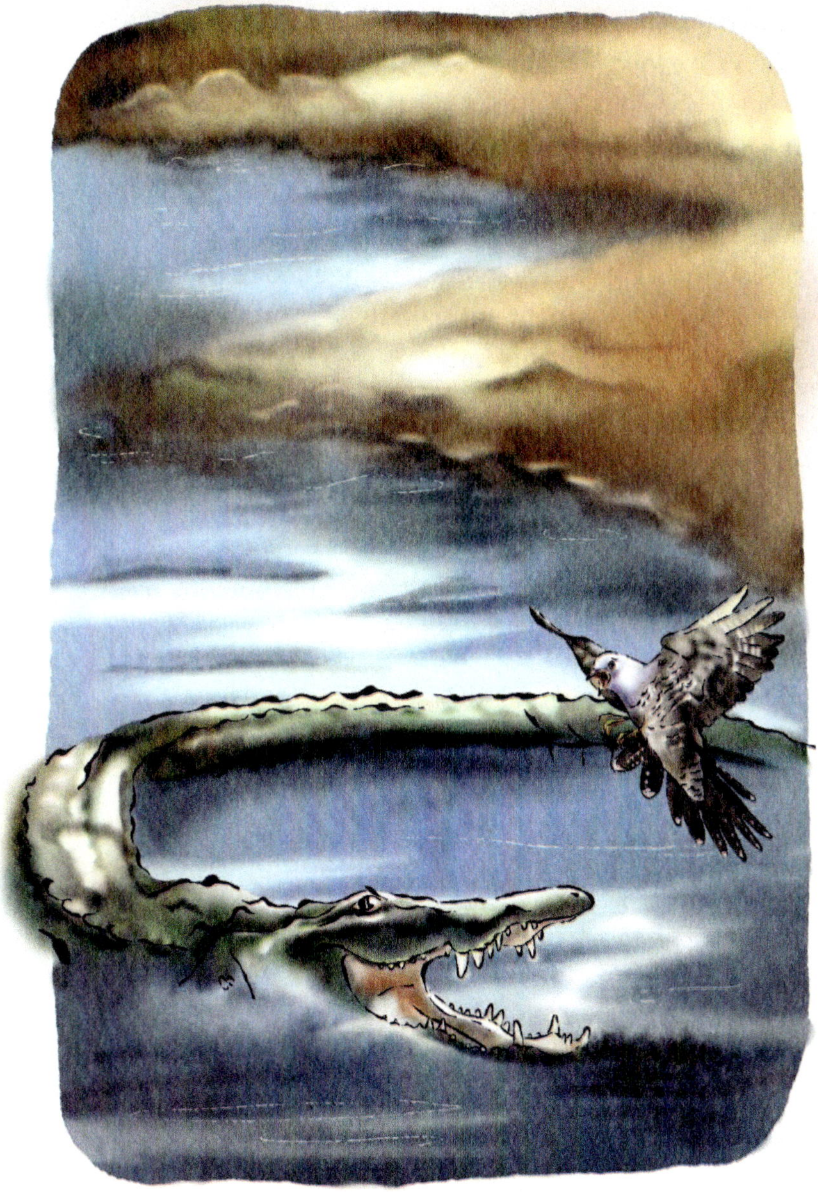

THUMP, THUMP, THUMP, the branches shook underneath his feet and Tick-tock was instantly awake. "What on earth?" he thought to himself as he looked around. It didn't take long for him to see the giant grey elephants walking past his tree. Tick-Tock stretched his wings, he had not had much sleep and the thought of resting the whole day made him even more tired. Watching the large grey beasts move along, he thought to himself that they were actually moving in the direction he needed to fly. Tick-Tock thought for a moment, and then flew up into the air and landed on the elephants back.

"Hello?" the elephant asked.

"Hello, my name is Tick-Tock, what's your name?" Tick-Tock asked.

"Freddie, Freddie Blue and not to be rude but why have you landed on my back?" Freddie asked.

"Well Freddie, I had quite a traumatic experience yesterday, I almost became lunch so I didn't get much sleep through the night and now I'm so tired. However I need to keep moving and you're going in my direction so I wondered if I might catch a ride with you?" Tick-Tock enquired.

Freddie stopped and thought for a moment….."well Tick-Tock, nothing comes for free so if you scratch my back, I'll scratch yours perhaps……as the saying goes." He chuckled.

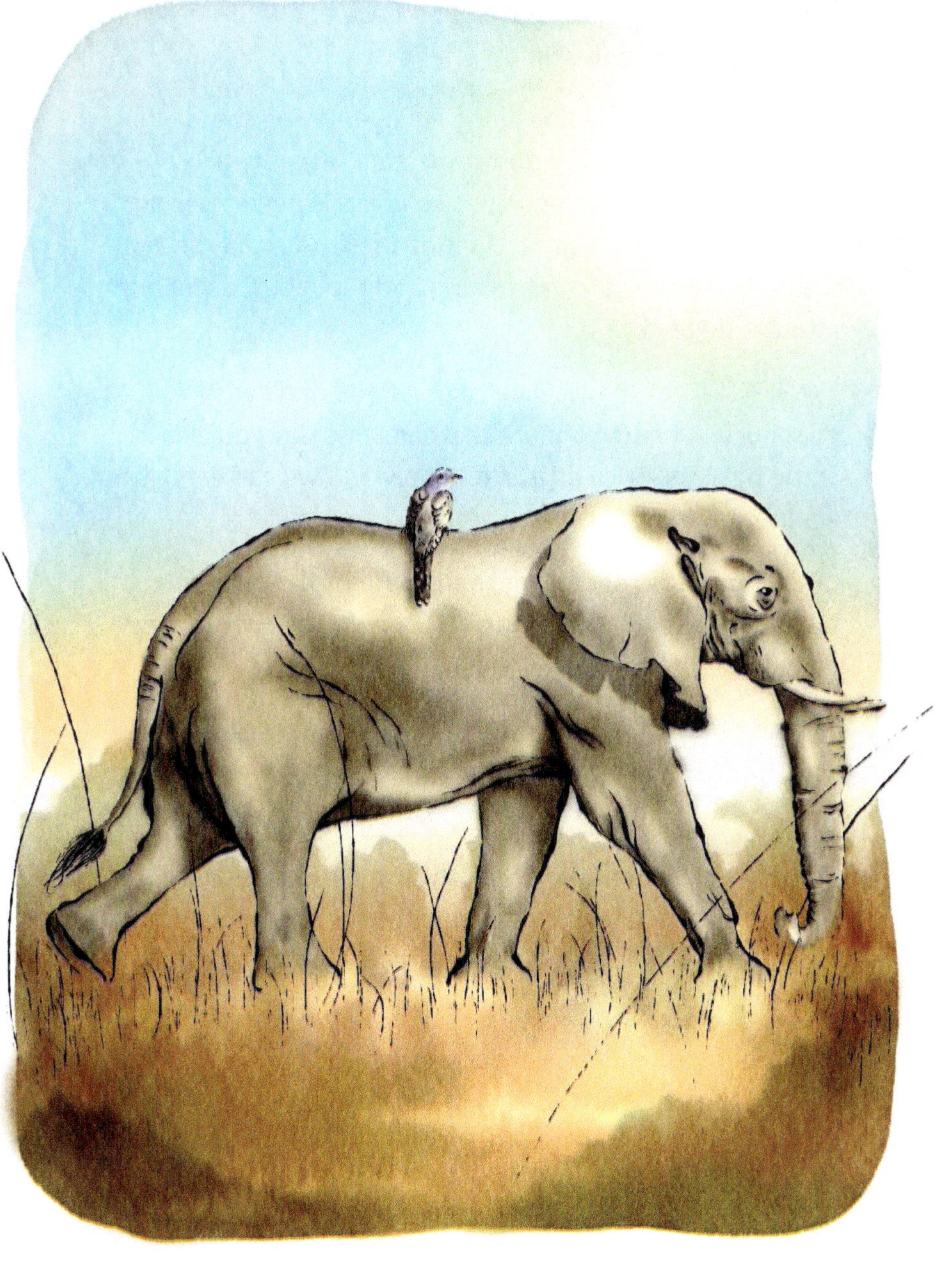

"Scratch your back? Oh yes I can do that as I've got nice long claws." Tick-Tock replied and began to walk and dig into Freddie's rough skin.

Freddie began thumping along again enjoying the sensation as he walked under the sun. After a while, curious about each other the two animals began talking, telling each other their fascinating life stories and before they knew it the sun was setting and the moon rising high into the night sky.

"Well Tick-Tock, it was nice to meet you and I wish you good luck in finding a mate. Perhaps one day you can come back to Africa as a little family and we can catch up again." Freddie said as he came to a stop by a tree.

"Yes I hope so Freddie and thank you for the ride, you have been most helpful in my journey" Tick-Tock replied flying up to a branch.

"Remember, you scratch my back and I'll scratch yours little bird" Freddie said, chuckling to himself as he walked away.

Tick-Tock looked around him, this was Africa, he had finally made it. Closing his eyes, he went to sleep content.

Chapter 9

"Good morning little bird, good morning" purred a leopard to Tick-Tock.

Tick-Tock opened his eyes and stretched. "Good morning Mr leopard, good morning." he replied.

"You know the earth is soft under my paws and I bet there are lots of yummy worms, let me dig into it for you and you can hop down and have some breakfast" the leopard called up.

Tick-Tock looked down at the leopard and suddenly got an uneasy feeling, "why are you offering to help me Mr Leopard?" Tick-Tock asked.

"Please call me Mike, and I'm just trying to be nice." Mike the leopard said.

"Well, you're stretching my back how will I scratch yours? I bet you're hoping I will be your breakfast?!"

Mike laughed, "you're silly little bird are you little bird, such a shame as I'm feeling rather peckish" he said as he walked away.

Definitely I must keep my wits about me thought Tick-Tock and with that, he began to fly around and look at his new temporary home. As he flew around looking for waterholes and good spots for food, he also noticed all the other cuckoo birds hanging around. He wondered which one of them, if any, could be the ONE, the one who would understand, the one who would be his mate.

The next few weeks went by and although Tick-Tock had talked to many different cuckoos, none of them quite got it or understood how he felt. Some tried too, but most thought his idea was absurd. Raise their young themselves? Ruin their good looks and waste their time…..for what? Squawking babies that just steal all the food? No, that could never be.

As Tick-Tock perched on a tree feeling disheartened and lonely he noticed a cuckoo beneath him searching for food on the ground. He thought she was a pretty little thing to look at and watched her hunt for her breakfast. Then Tick-Tock noticed a large shape in the grass in front of her and that uneasy feeling was back again so Tick-Tock dived down towards her shouting "JUMP! FLY AWAY! QUICK! QUICK!" Swerving before he hit the ground, all Tick-Tock could see was a large animal about to pounce on them. "LEFT, LEFT, FLY LEFT!" he yelled and they both darted left missing the creature by mere seconds. Then up they flew onto the branch and looked down to see what was hunting them.

"That's the second time you've escaped being my breakfast little bird" Mike said with a huff. "Yes, and that's the second time you've tried to eat me." Tick-Tock replied. "Well, I've got to eat and you're my food, it is what it is little bird" Mike said coldly. "You could change that, but I guess it's useless trying to ask a leopard to change it's spots" Tick-Tock replied. "Some things will never change" Mike said as he walked away.

"Oh wow, you're truly my hero, you just saved my life" the cuckoo exclaimed to Tick-Tock. "Well, it was nothing really, I just did what any cuckoo would do." Tick-Tock replied modestly. "I'm not sure about that, I've been here a few weeks and everyone I've met has been so rude to me, no one would share their feeding spots, everyone just looking out for themselves. I've felt so scared and lonely, I'm just not used to it. Growing up, my family always shared everything with each other." the cuckoo told him looking quite upset. "My family was the same, we looked out for each other and shared what we had" Tick-Tock replied.

He sat looking at her and knew, this was his one, this was the cuckoo that would understand and so he introduced himself and she told him her name was Moema, but he could call her Mo. They started to get to know each other, he listened to how she had been raised by magpies and like him, felt no different from her family. Tick-Tock told her about his family and his brother and the incident that had happened. He told her about the farm animals, the owl and they talked for hours, which turned into days,

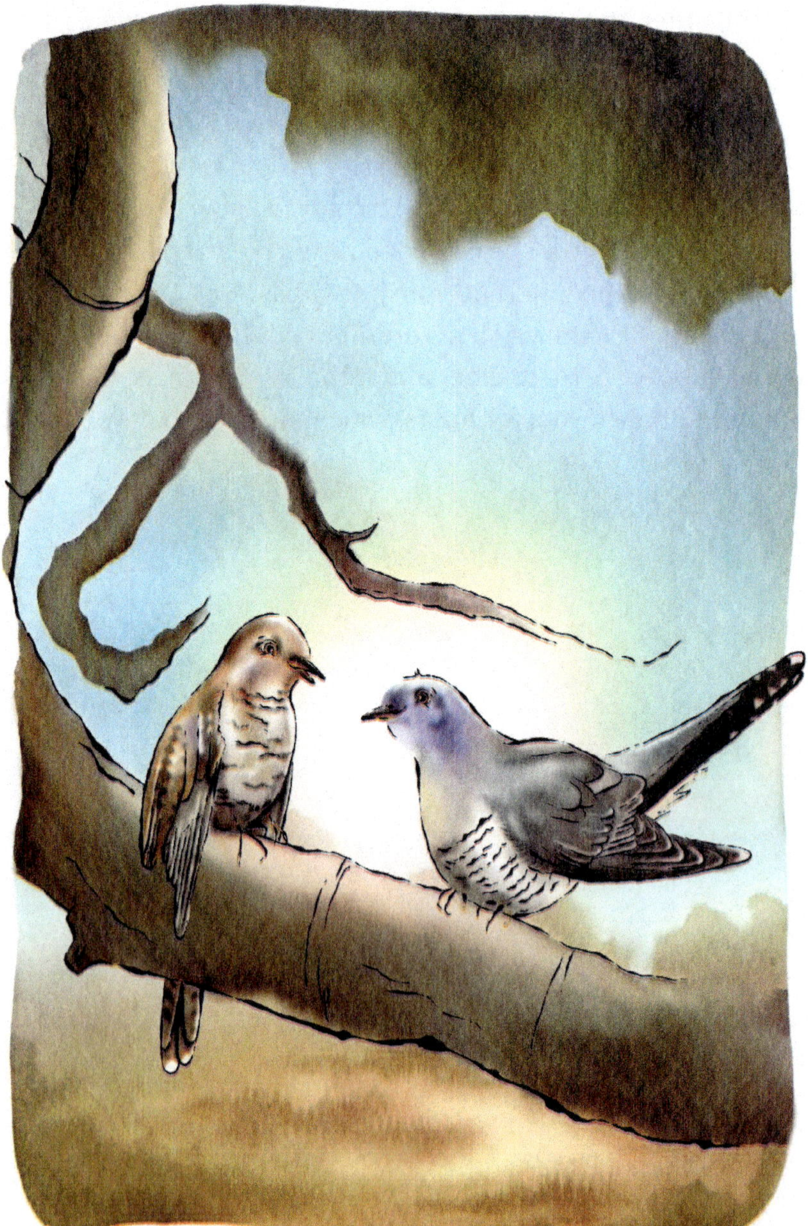

which then turned into weeks. Eventually, Tick-Tock asked her what he felt was the most important question.

"So, would you do it? Would you abandon your eggs?" he asked. "Well, I don't know, in my heart I want to but in my head the thought of raising them is scary, it would be a lot of work and very tiring, I know I couldn't do it without someone by my side but that someone is hard to find. To make this work, you need to be kind and loving, you need to be able to work together and compromise and cuckoos…..at least the ones I've met so far….. they don't seem to get this or want this." Mo explained.

"I would do it with you, you and I are so alike in the way we were raised and the way we think. We could do it, we could be different and have a family and live together happily." Tick-Tock told her.

Mo looked at the little bird who she was slowly falling in love with, she felt safe and loved and knew in her heart that he had a good soul and would make an excellent father.

"Yes, I think perhaps we could." Mo replied.

Chapter 10

Whilst all this was happening in Africa, Titch had been getting stronger and stronger living with the humans. The little girl doted over him everyday and fed him the biggest worms she could find, he no longer looked like such a frail little thing and his wing was fully healed. He enjoyed living there, it was warm and he was loved, but he missed his family and felt saddened that they had never come to find him. Perhaps they didn't know where to look? Or perhaps they thought he had died.

As Titch sat there eating his breakfast, Bernie came to the table as usual with his coffee, but no newspaper today. He gave Titch's head a little scratch and turned to look at Sky. "Now love, I know you've grown quite fond of your little Robin but he is well and truly better now, his wing is healed and you've fattened him up good and proper. It's time he goes out in the wild and finds a mate." Bernie said.

"Oh but dad, do I have to? He's happy here he doesn't need a mate" Sky said sadly.

"Of course, he does Sky, everyone needs to find their special someone in life. It's the right thing to do and I want it done after breakfast please" Bernie told her.

Sky slouched over in her chair saddened at the thought of losing her little robin. "Now now love, it's okay, robins are loving and loyal creatures, he will come back and visit and probably even bring his family to say hello." Shelia said whilst comforting her daughter.

So Sky finished her breakfast and carried Titch outside. She nuzzled into his little head and gave him a kiss. "Goodbye my little Robin, please come back and visit because I am really going to miss you" she told him. Then she stretched out her arms and gently tossed him up so he would fly.

"Goodbye my little human Sky, and thank you for everything" Titch called to her as he flew away.

he had left he had been so small he couldn't even fly and everything looked the same. He wasn't sure what he was going to do now, he missed his family but would they still be here in these woods and how would he find them?

Titch flew around for what seemed like forever and then went down to a little lake for a drink where he sat for a while and thought about what to do. Should he try to find his family or should he find his mate and have his own. As he was thinking to himself, he noticed another robin sitting on the opposite bank and noticed how stunning she was. Was this his opportunity? Was fate telling him what he needed to do?

He remembered asking his dad how he met his mum, Henry had told him that he brought her the biggest worm he could find, dropped it by her feet and then stepped back and waited patiently. Patience was the key he said, you need to give them time to look at you properly and admire your stunning feathers. So Titch looked around him and started digging into the soil to find the perfect worm. Then he flew over the lake with it and placed it by her feet, he stepped back and waited.

The robin looked at the worm, It was fat and juicy and looked delicious. She then looked at Titch, he was also quite chubby, he had beautiful feathers and a kind face. She sat and thought how good he must be at finding food, he looked strong and was clearly confident enough to fly over here so she decided to give him a chance.

"Josephine, that's my name, but I mostly get called Jo" She told him. "Hello Jo, I've mostly been called Robin but I prefer the name Titch." Titch replied. "Titch?" Jo laughed "there's nothing tiny about you" She said. "Ahh well, I used to be, it's a family nickname and it's all I've got left of them really, I lost them in these woods when I was younger." Titch explained. "Oh that's sad, you know I saw an older pair of robins as I was flying around just yesterday, the only pair of robins I've seen all week to be honest. Not sure who they were but I could take you to them if you like?" Jo told him. "That would be wonderful Jo, perhaps it's my parents or maybe they know my family and know what happened to them!" Titch replied, feeling so happy at the thought of being reunited.

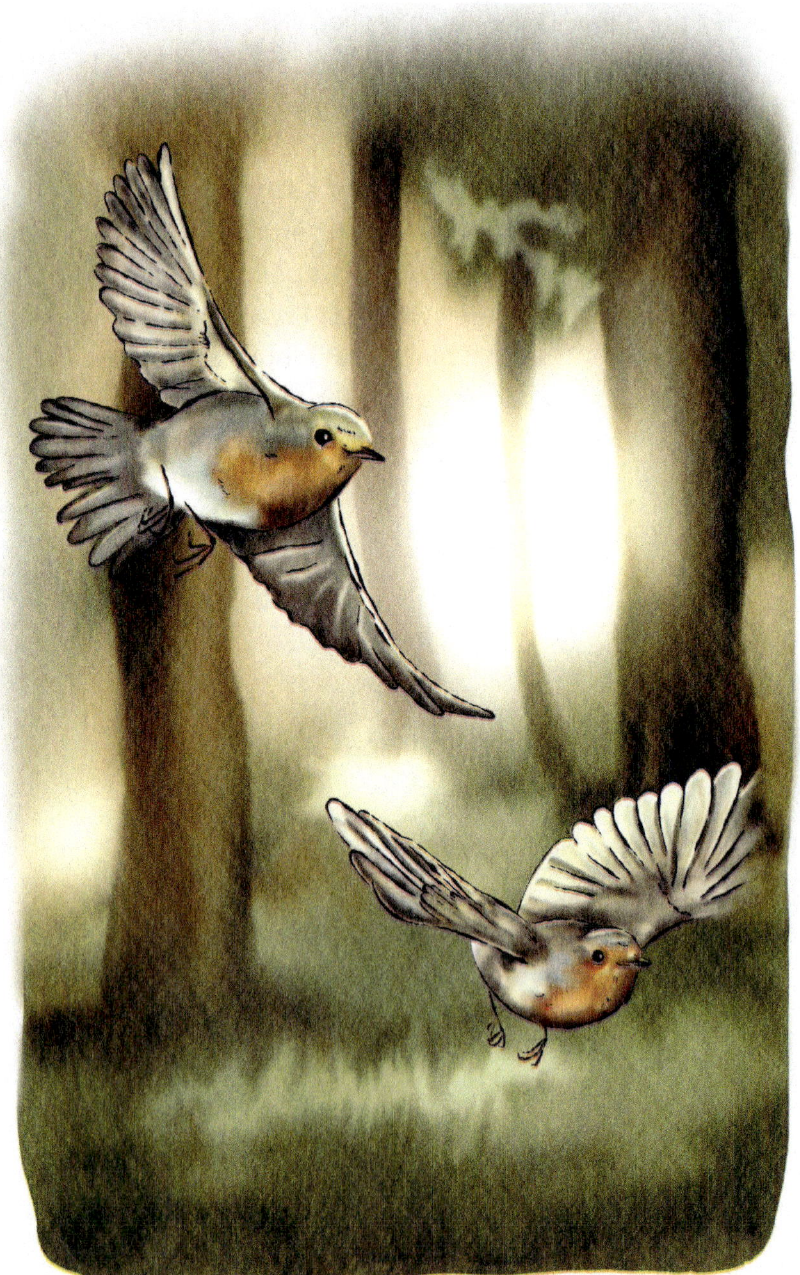

So Titch followed Jo and on the way, they got to know each other a bit more. Titch told her about his brother and his accident and the farmhouse. Jo told Titch about her life, how she lived in a little village tree but loved going to different woods to explore them, to look for the perfect place that could be her forever home. After a while Titch started to recognise his surroundings, he felt sure they were just surrounded by any old trees but then there was something about these trees that felt familiar and then he spotted it and he knew straight away. It was his nest, it was his childhood home and inside sat his mother.

Racing forward, Titch yelled "Mum,Mum!"as he flew into the nest and nuzzled his head against hers. "Titch? Oh my little boy, just look at you! Oh, I'm so happy to see you my love" Ruby exclaimed nuzzling his head back. Ruby stepped back and took a look at her now fully grown child. "Just look at you! Not so small anymore are you? Your father will be back any minute with some food and then you must tell us everything, but first, who is this with you?" Ruby asked.

"This is Jo, she's amazing, she helped me find you!" Titch told his mum smiling.

"Oh, I don't know about amazing" Jo laughed modestly. "You are truley amazing Jo for bringing our boy home, it's lovely to meet you" Ruby replied.

Titch could see another robin flying towards the nest and as he got closer and closer, he recognised his dad. As soon as he perched himself down, Titch gave him a hug. "Oh, dad I've missed you so much, I missed both of you so much." Titch cried. "Titch, Titch is that really you son, look at how much you've grown! You must tell us everything!" Henry said.

So Titch told them about the farmhouse and Sky, he told them how he had broken his wing and that they had bandaged it for him. He told them how Sky had fed him the biggest worms to fatten him up and although he had felt loved and safe, he had missed his family dearly. Ruby and Henry explained to Titch that his brother had gone looking for him, they told him they knew he was safe and being looked after but thought of him every day. They told him about his brother and how he had visited the owl and been given the name Tick-Tock, how he was now in Africa and intended to be different and raise his own family. Then Henry and Ruby got to know Jo and heard of her life, her family and how she lived in the nearest village. They thanked her again for helping Titch find them and reuniting them as a family. The robins talked and talked for hours laughing and crying and enjoying each others company.

"You know I must really be heading back to my nest" Jo told Titch. "Well let me fly you back, I insist, after how much you've helped me, I want to see you home safe." Titch told her.

So off they flew towards the village whilst chatting some more, but this time they talked about the future and all their dreams and plans. When they arrived at the nest her family were all sleeping.

"You know, today has probably been one of the best days of my life and it's all down to you Jo. Do you think maybe we could plan a future together? Titched asked. "We both want a family and you said you loved exploring the woods, we could build a nest and live there." Titch said excitedly.

"Well if this is a proposal, should you not be down on one knee?" Jo laughed as she looked adoringly at Titch.

So down on one knee Titch went, "Josephine, would you do me the honour of becoming my mate?" Titch asked.

"Yes, I would love to" Jo replied beaming with joy. "You can stay the night and tomorrow we will go back to the woods and build our own nest together." Jo said.

So Titch and Jo perched together in the nest talking and planning their future and eventually fell asleep.

Chapter 11

Meanwhile back in Africa Tick-Tock and Mo had grown closer and closer. They knew they were exactly what each other wanted and were preparing to make the long journey back to settle down and raise their family. After a few days of eating and sleeping to build their strength, they set of for England.

As they flew through the skies, they chatted about their future together, the things they needed to do and organise before the little one would arrive. As Mo and Tick-Tock looked ahead they could see something, "what's that? Is it storm clouds?" Mo asked struggling to see. "No, it's worse than that, it's a plague of locusts, we're in for a bumpy ride. Keep flying straight and look down but forward, hopefully it will be over quick." Tick-Tock replied.

So in the two birds went, heads down and flying straight, getting hit by locusts and knocked about. After about five minutes they were both exhausted. "Tick-Tock this is too tiring, we can't get through this, we've not even flown a mile and I'm covered in bruises" Mo cried out. "Yes love, your right! Let's just fly down to the ground, we can find some food and recover." Tick-Tock replied.

So down the birds flew and as they got closer to the ground, Tick-Tock noticed some termite mounds. "We chose a good spot, there's plenty of food here love" he said. "Let's rest on these low branches and then when we wake up we can have a little feast" Mo said.

The two birds woke up startled, they could hear a scratching noise and a low growl. The day had gotten darker but they could just make out a figure by the termite mounds. Tick-Tock flew up and hovered over the animal but still couldn't make out what it was but after a couple of minutes the creature stopped digging and looked up at Tick-Tock. "Hello, I suppose you'll be wanting some of these termites little bird," the animal said. "Yes, that was the plan" Tick-Tock chuckled, "how have you managed to dig in there so deep? You must have very strong legs and sharp claws." Tick-Tock stated. "Well yes of course, I'm an aardvark, we're born with the right tool to get the job done, otherwise we'd probably starve." The aardvark replied.

"Oh, you're an aardvark! Sorry it's hard to see in this light. Well, I'm glad you came along, it would have taken me hours to get to the centre myself. When you're full, my mate and I will come and have a bite." said Tick-Tock.

"You're quite welcome to perch down and eat now as I mean you no harm, I doubt you taste anywhere near as good as these little creatures" the aardvark said with a chuckle.

66

So Tick-Tock and Mo flew down onto the termite mound for a feast and after a good meal and chat they started back on their journey.

Eventually they made it to Morocco, flying through most of the night and coming up to the midday sun both the birds were hot and tired. "Down here, look there's a little pool of water" Mo said flying towards it. "Good spot, I'm parched and tired so let's get a drink and find some shade to rest in."

As they got closer, they noticed the area was quite populated with humans, but they didn't mind. They sat themselves on the edge and started guzzling at the water.

A little girl who was sitting close by noticed them, "look mummy, look! There are two little birds by the pond" she said pointing at them. "Can I feed them some bread?" She asked her mum.

"Yes of course, they are migrating birds and must be hungry on their long journey," her mother replied. "What's a migrating bird?" the little girl asked as she ripped up some bread in her lap. "It means every year in the winter when their home is cold, they fly away to where it is hot….like a holiday," her mother explained. "Oh, that sounds nice! We should do that too," the little girl replied laughing.

She got up and not wanting to frighten them, she walked slowly towards the two birds, she then tossed the bread over trying to get it as close to their feet as she could.

"Oh, lucky us, look at this little girl giving us some food" said Tick-Tock as he hopped over to the breadcrumbs. "Yes, todays meal needs no work" Mo said laughing. The two birds ate up all the bread then flew up into a palm tree for a shaded rest.

Waking up at sunset they set of again, flying all through the night and eventually reaching Paris.

"Oh, it's the city of love." Mo said excitedly.

"Yes, but it's also the city of pigeons" Tick-Tock chuckled. "I say we fly straight over and go to the countryside, there will be a better chance of finding some grubs there" said Tick-Tock. "Very well" Mo replied and so they continued flying past the Eiffel Tower into the countryside of France.

As they flew on, they started to notice lots of fields, farmers' fields. "Let's stop somewhere nearby, it's Spring and the farmers are going to be ploughing these fields and that will bring up all the worms and grubs" Tick-Tock said. So, they flew down and perched in a large tree, they rested and waited. Sure enough, within a few days the farmers were out with their big machines ploughing up all the fields getting them ready. When they were done and gone the two birds flew down and ate up the biggest worms they could find, filling their tummies for the last part of their journey.

In the morning they set of again, heading for Dover in England. It didn't take long for them to get there and with such a picturesque view they thought it might be nice to spend the day just relaxing.

"This is just beautiful isn't it, sitting here in the breeze with the view of the ocean. This is what life is about" said Mo.

"It really is, it's just so peaceful" Tick-Tock replied.

As if the universe had heard them, in that exact moment a shadow cast over the two birds and above them a peregrine falcon was diving towards them. "JUMP!" Tick-Tock yelled and they both dived off the cliff towards the ocean. Down and down they went, frantically scanning for safety. As the falcon was getting closer and closer Mo noticed a small alcove in the cliff and sped towards it. "This way!" She shouted and with not a moment to spare they both dived deep into the alcove landing roughly.

"Oh no, I've gone and got us trapped, what are we going to do? How are we going to get out?" Mo said frantically.

"No, it's okay, this is a good spot, we will just have to wait it out until nightfall and hope he gets bored." Tick-Tock replied trying to stay calm. "Honestly women, you're bad luck you are, leopards, locusts and now a peregrine falcon. You've got as many lives as a cat!" Tick-Tock said jokingly, trying to lighten the mood. "Don't, I am bad luck, but you must be my lucky charm keeping us safe." Mo replied.

The two birds waited quietly until late into the night. They had heard the falcon fly away after a few hours, it had realised the alcove was to narrow to reach them and they had not heard it return since.

Chapter 12

"Okay, the plan is too stick to the cliff. There are lots of little alcoves we can go into if the falcon is waiting, we will fly right down to the shore so it's harder for it to see us and we'll fly along the coast. I remember when I was young and practicing my flying, if I went up high above the tree tops I could see the cliffs so we must be close to the woods. It shouldn't take too long before we get to our new home." Tick-Tock explained.

So the birds set off, they dropped down the cliff and flew along the edge. Soon the cliffs were well behind them and they were flying along coastal villages. Feeling safe the falcon was gone, they flew up over the rooftops and kept going until they reached a farmhouse, some plough fields and finally a beautiful wood.

Tick-Tock led the way through the trees until finally he saw a nest with robins. Thinking it was his parents as there had never been any other robins around, he went and landed straight on the nest without a second thought.

So when a bird screamed and started to attack him, he was very much caught by surprise. "No, go away you bully, you won't have my eggs" the little Robin shouted, hitting out at them both. "Titch! Titch! Come Quick!" The robin screamed.

Tick-Tock and Mo quickly jumped off the nest and flew away to a tree close by. "Little Robin, I'm so sorry, please don't be scared" Tick-Tock shouted towards the nest. "You called for Titch, Titch is my brother, I thought this nest belonged to my parents, oh I'm so sorry to have scared you."

Titch having heard the commotion, came flying over just in time to hear Tick-Tock shouting over. He flew towards him and gave him a hug. "Oh, bruv, it's so good to see you! Jo come here, don't worry it's only Tick-Tock." Titch said beckoning his mate over. "Titch, the eggs, I can't leave the nest but its lovely to meet you Tick-Tock, I'm so sorry for attacking you, I didn't know it was you and I was taken by surprise at the way you just appeared on the nest," Jo called out. "Oh, don't be sorry, I'm the one who's sorry for scaring you!" Tick-Tock replied.

"So, Titch, I'd like you to meet Mo and I'd love for Mum and Dad to meet her, where are they?" Tick-Tock asked. "This way, follow me" Titch answered taking flight.

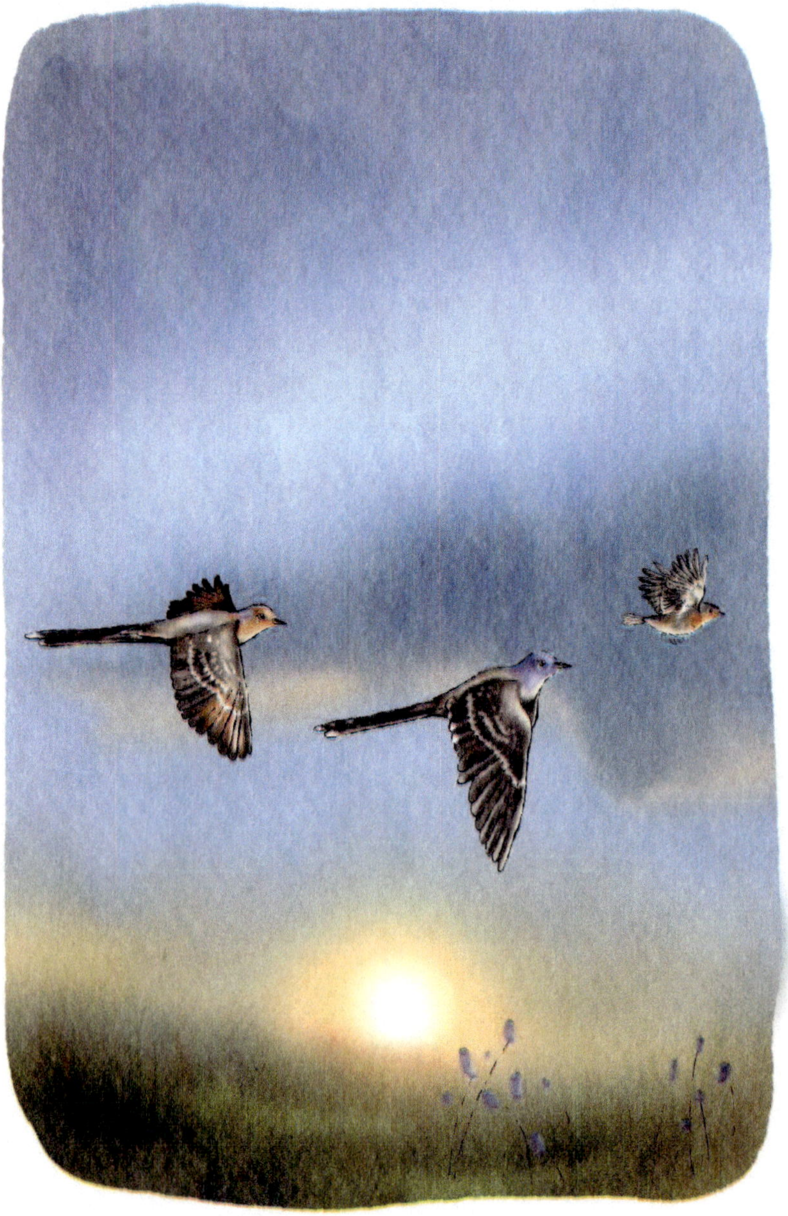

"Mum, Dad!" Tick-Tock exclaimed going to hug his parents. "It's so good to see you both, I've missed you so much."

"It's so good to see you too my love, look at our two boys together again, and who's this?" Ruby asked.

"This is Mo she's about to have eggs and we came here to build a nest and raise them, just like I said I would Mum" Tick-Tock answered. "Actually Dad and Titch, would you both help me? Mo Is exhausted, she is so close to laying and I want to build the perfect nest as soon as possible but I'm not even sure where to start" Tick-Tock said.

So the three birds worked together and by sundown had built a beautiful soft nest near to his parents and brother. They had spent the time catching up, reminiscing and talking about what the future may hold.

"It's getting late, I'm going to go back to the missus with some grub, I'm so happy to say I'll see you in the morning bruv. It's honestly so good to have you home." said Titch before he took flight to his nest.

Sitting alongside his Dad with Mo asleep next to him, Tick-Tock felt so content with his life. "I know I sometimes treated you a bit differently growing up Tick-Tock, it wasn't intentional and I hated myself for it. Please know how much I love you and how proud I am of who you have become. You have fought against your nature to become a father and raise a family and you are going to be such a good dad, I can't wait to see what the future holds for you." Henry said.

"Thank you, dad. I'm so excited for my future too"

The End.

Printed in Great Britain
by Amazon